This Little Tiger book belongs to:

_____

_____

_____

For my good friend Joan — C. F.

For Jeff, for your love and encouragement — A. E.

LITTLE TIGER PRESS
1 The Coda Centre, 189 Munster Road, London SW6 6AW
www.littletigerpress.com

First published in Great Britain 2007
by Little Tiger Press, London
This edition published 2012

Printed in China

2 4 6 8 10 9 7 5 3 1

Follow That Bear
If You DARE!

Claire Freedman

Alison Edgson

LITTLE TIGER PRESS

Hare loved bears.
He liked big bears, little bears,
hairy bears, and scary bears.
   "If only I could find a bear,"
said Hare. "If only I could catch one!
The hairier and scarier the better!"

So Hare bought a book: *The Best Book of Bear Hunting*. He opened his book and took a look.

"Rabbit!" called Hare. "I need you
for a Very Important Bear Hunt!"
"A Bear Hunt?" said Rabbit. "How
do you hunt for bears?"
"It's all in my book," explained Hare. So he
turned the page, and they took a look.

STEP 2

THINGS YOU WILL NEED

To catch your bear,
take a fishing net,
some string — as long as
you can get —

	L	S	D
	20	0	0
	10	5	2
	0	2	4
	30	7	6

A LIGHT to shine
deep inside his lair,
and watchful eyes ~

BEARS LURK EVERYWHERE!

"Are you sure you want to find a bear, Hare?" said Rabbit.

"Of course!" Hare said. "The hairier and scarier the better! Look, I've found a fishing net, a flashlight, and a piece of string. What's next?"

They turned another page in Hare's book and took a look.

STEP 3

TRAILING YOUR BEAR

Now bears are not always easily found, so look out for pawprints on the ground.

Crouch down low but please beware — THE BIGGER THE PAWPRINT, THE BIGGER THE BEAR!

"I don't think I like the sound of Bear Hunting," said Rabbit anxiously. "I hope we don't find any bear prints!"

"Over here!" called Hare excitedly. "I've found some!"

"Oh, dear!" said Rabbit. "They must belong to a VERY hairy, scary bear. Now what?"

They turned another page of Hare's
book and took a look.

STEP 4

WHAT TO LOOK OUT FOR

BEARS like to scratch on a special tree, it sharpens their claws quite nastily.

THEIR nails stay as sharp as the teeth in their jaws.

The deeper the scratch marks, the sharper the claws!

"I really don't like the idea of Bear Hunting!"
cried Rabbit. "Let's go back!"

"Not now!" cried Hare excitedly. "We're
on the trail! And look what I've found!"

Rabbit looked. "Oh, no!" he cried.
"Now what do we do?"

"I'll tell you," said Hare. "It's all in my book."

So they turned another page
and took a look.

HIDE yourself quickly
and take great care—
the louder the rumble,
the hungrier the bear!

Rumble Grumble!

"Shh! Did you hear that?" whispered Hare excitedly. "That sounds like a very hungry bear to me!"

"Hear it?" trembled Rabbit. "I was almost deafened by it! Quick, Hare, let's take another look in your book!"

"Yikes!" gulped Rabbit. "Look
over there, Hare!"

"Where?"

"It's a BEAR!"

"HELP! We'll never catch HIM with a fishing net
and a piece of string!" trembled Rabbit.
"Just watch me try!" cried Hare.
"I'm HUNGRY!" growled the bear.
Then, suddenly…

"Dinner's ready," called Mommy Bear.

"It's bear-sized beans on bear-sized toast."

"Yummy!" said Little Bear.

"Come back!" called Hare.
Poor Rabbit was too weak to speak!
"Oh, no," cried Hare. "I can't lose
my bear—that's not fair!"

Quickly he took another look in his book.

STEP 7

WHAT BEARS LIKE TO EAT

A HUNGRY bear with an appetite will eat up any food in sight.

And all bears hate baked beans on toast

But love ripe hares and rabbits the most!

Rabbit quickly grabbed
Hare's paw.
"Run for it, Hare! It's lucky those
bears have never read your book.
For if they did, I bet they'd try to make
a hare and rabbit pie!"